HELLO FRIEND..

Do you want to make this book yours?

HURRY UP and write your name **HERE**

........Leo...

.............Thanks JAedon...............

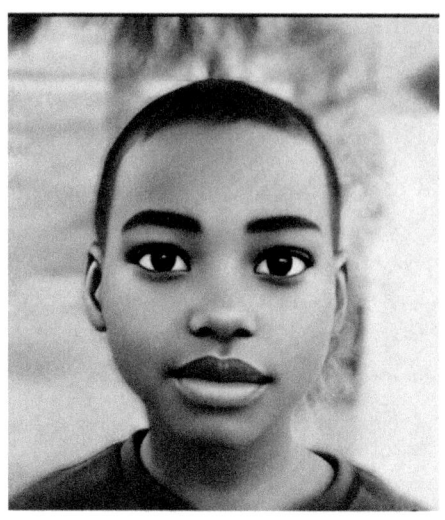

JOHN OFON was born and raised in the economic capital of Cameroon but now lives in southwest London, adjoining the River Thames. Between the ages of 8 and 10, John estimates having read over 200 books in both the fiction and nonfiction genres. His passion for words and storytelling was first noticed by his English teacher in year 4, Mr. Hosam. And only a year later, John decided to translate his passion into his first book, which has four unique bedtime stories for children.

Instead of playing video games, John always finds himself under the covers in his room with his laptop, developing his storylines and translating his wild imagination into creative writing.

His desire to become a well-read author across the globe was recently reinforced by his year 5 English teacher, Ms. Walmsley, and John decided to launch his first book series **"FIVE BEASTS."**.

WORLD, BE ON YOUR TOES AND LOOK OUT FOR THIS 10-YEAR-OLD AUTHOR AS HE DEBUTS HIS WRITING CAREER.

Books by John Ofon

Unique Tales

Gold Tales

FIVE BEASTS

JOHN OFON

Young and Independent Ltd Children's Books

London, United Kingdom
GU16 8XE

First published in Great Britain by YAI, an imprint of
YoungAndIndependent Ltd 2023
Copyright © John Ofon 2023

Children's Books

Dedicated to my English teachers Ms Emma Walmsley and Mr Hosam Jabri

Thank you for inspiring and encouraging me to pursue my passion for writing.

Table of Contents

PART ONE

ICE

CHAPTER ONE

DOWN THE

DITCH

Kevin Glacier had been playing in his snowy garden when a huge roar lured him out into the open.

He could not see what it was, but it was a tall, white-coated shape that was at least ten metres taller than him.

Kevin slowly withdrew a tiny slingshot from his pocket.

He then shot a little stone directly at the belly
of the beast.

It hit the beast hard, and a low growl could be
heard as Kevin backed away.

The creature dashed at him, and the boy took off running. He didn't know where they were, but he just ran.

A huge fist stroked hard against his back, and Kevin could feel himself rolling down a snowy hill.

As soon as he opened his eyes, he cried out loud, "I'm going to roll into a ditch!" The boy tried to stop himself from rolling further, but he just went faster and faster.

Eventually, he fell into the hole.

He looked up, and a pair of sharp, red eyes were staring down at him.

CHAPTER TWO

THE FIRST BEAST

Kevin got up and ran.

He could hear the deafening sound of the beast landing in the ditch.

He drew up into a stony ancient corridor and looked over to the wall on the left. On the wall, there were five different angles of the kingdom of **MYSTERIA**; fire, ice, water, rock, and wind.

Kevin's awareness tingled. He turned around to see an old man dressed top to bottom in blue.

"Kevin, he said. It is your destiny to find the ice beast and bring him back to the ice mountain. I believe you have had an encounter with him.

His name is Julius, and he is the beast who used to protect your Ice Kingdom.

Without the beast, the ice village will remain unprotected, which is why we need you to bring him back. And with that, the man disappeared. Kevin heard a familiar growl,

and <u>in</u> a flash, Julius jumped at the poor boy. As Kevin dodged, an idea flashed into his mind.

He took off running, and as he turned the corner, a flight of steps stood there as if by magic.

Kevin grinned and ran up the stairs and into the snowy peaks, with Julius close behind. The boy spotted a huge gate—his village!

CHAPTER THREE

JULIUS

Kevin pushed past his village gate as he ran straight into his village's armour shop. Scrambling through the items on the shelves, he quickly grabbed a chest armour.

Outside the shop, his village army was trying everything within their powers to ward off Julius the beast.

Kevin quickly geared up and dashed out to face his destiny.

Kevin watched as Julius disposed of the soldiers one by one. He noticed that there was a little scratch on Julius's arm.

Julius roared. Kevin slowly walked towards him, but the beast didn't move. He slowly touched Julius's snout, then he pulled a little ribbon out of his bag.

Kevin gently tied the ribbon around Julius's arm, and the beast's red eyes suddenly turned bright blue. He gently stood up and walked slowly back towards the gate. The guards got up and looked directly at Kevin.

Julius turned around and gave a light wave.
Kevin waved back, and to his surprise, the
beast had disappeared. The whole town looked
back to see Julius on top of the mountain
peak, finger in mouth.

PART TWO

FIRE

CHAPTER FOUR

THE VOLCANO

Pyro Blaze was having the best time of his life. Growing up in a fire-infested kingdom, the boy had always felt bored. All he ever ate was flame sauce, the hottest chili in the galaxy.

But today was his birthday, and he had begged his protective parents if he could go lava surfing in Haggus, the hottest volcano on the island. "Fine," Dad had said. "You can go just this time." Pyro had rushed out of his house, grabbed his board, and surfed off into the sea of lava. "I've got to explore more!" Pyro said.

Suddenly, he heard the sound of hooves. He looked to his right, and saw a winged horse enveloped in fire galloping towards him. The horse immediately shot a ball of fire directly towards the edge of Pyro's board.

It snapped in half. "No!" cried the boy. In a fit of rage, he drew out his bow and aimed for the horse's side. As soon as it touched the horse, the arrow melted.

CHAPTER FIVE

THE SECOND

BEAST

Pyro found himself on the ground, unable to recall what had happened. He opened his eyes to see the blurry figure of a winged horse staring at him intently. The horse seemed fixated on one thing in particular, and Pyro soon realized that his mother's pendant was

shining emerald green on his chest, seemingly
hypnotizing the inflamed beast.

Slowly rising to his feet, Pyro reached out to
touch the pendant. Suddenly, a mysterious
hologram of a person appeared before him.
"Hello, young Pyro," the hologram boomed.

The horse you have encountered is called Zeta, the guardian of the fire kingdom.

Unfortunately, she has been separated from her kingdom due to a major event. You must lead her back to King Blade's kingdom, where she will reunite with her people.

With those words, the hologram disappeared, and Pyro couldn't help but grin in excitement.

CHAPTER SIX

ZETA

Pyro found himself riding Zeta like a noble knight. The people back in **FLAMETOPIA** were befuddled to see a boy riding the legendary guardian.

"Son?" exclaimed a befuddled dad. "You can have the pendant now, buddy," said the boy, giving the horse a pat.

As much as he tried to ignore the pain, he couldn't help but perform a series of backflips and yelps. "Ow!" he cried.

Much to his embarrassment, the crowd watching him roared with laughter. Pyro blushed tomato red. However, the crowd still looked upon him and his new stallion with respect, seeing him as a hero.

PART THREE

ROCK

CHAPTER SEVEN

THE BOULDER

Arnit Stone was charging at full strength. She was finally old enough to become a part of the "Boulders", the strongest **ROCKTOPIANS** of all time.

The age limit was twelve, and after a decade and two years of waiting, she could finally show off her strength.

Arnit smashed through the boulder as if it were spaghetti in her fingers, and the Boulders clapped in amazement. She then performed a deep curtsy.

"Why don't you try this boulder, Arnit?" said
the coach, pointing to a big cave with an even
bigger boulder blocking its entrance.

CHAPTER EIGHT

THE THIRD

BEAST

Arnit could hear the quiet chattering around her. She stepped over to the boulder.

"Many have tried, but none have succeeded, girl," said the coach. This wound Arnit up.

In a fit of rage, she charged at the boulder with all her strength. "En garde!" she shouted.

The amazed coach watched as a cloud of sparks flew into the air.

As the misty dust cleared, the "boulders" could see no block from the cave. Just Arnit standing there, looking into the cave.

She immediately ran into the cave. As she
looked around, she bumped into something.
Something big.

CHAPTER NINE

MIKA

The girl stood there, looking at the stony statue of a giant mammoth.

Suddenly, the outline of a mysterious man appeared behind her. "That is Mika," he said, "and you need to bring him back to the rock kingdom. To do so, you must unlock him." With that, he disappeared.

"How am I supposed to do that?" cried Arnit. She sighed, then stretched her arms into a pose and charged.

Like a little irritating fly, she was thrown back against the wall. She tried again and again, but nothing seemed to work. She could hear familiar, quiet chattering.

Arnit turned to see the whole team of "Boulders" staring at her. She turned around to face the mammoth again.

"En garde!" she screamed, charging fist first at the gigantic statue.

The statue shattered to pieces, and Mika opened his eyes slowly. The "Boulders" immediately backed away.

"Well, Arnit," the coach said, "welcome to the Boulders."

PART FOUR

WATER

CHAPTER TEN

THE BOTTLE

"Lia wave, come back here this second!" Aunt Sky called out to the girl.

Lia turned around and replied, "But Aunt Sky,
I..." "You forgot your coat, sweetheart,"
interrupted Mom, holding out a light blue
coat.

"Thanks," Lia said with a smile as she retrieved the coat. With a headfirst dive, she took off into the glistening ocean. "Whoo!" she exclaimed, being an expert swimmer. As she swam across the sea, she caught sight of something floating towards her.

"It's a message in a bottle!" cried the girl as she caught it in her hand.

However, as she was about to open it, something peculiar happened. "Aah!" she cried out as the strange bottle dragged her across the empty sea.

CHAPTER ELEVEN

THE FOURTH

BEAST

The bottle didn't take the girl far; it stopped abruptly in front of a giant bubble. Inside the bubble was a sleeping giant serpent.

As if by magic, the letter rolled itself out of the bottle and somehow remained dry. A booming voice echoed from it as if it were reading itself.

"Dear Lia," it said. "I believe my trusty magic letter has found you at a good time. I believe that pillow has also brought you to Uquo, the water serpent.

She used to protect the ocean but was trapped by a powerful bubble.

I believe you will find a way to release her
and save the ocean so your people can go back
to living in their ocean homes."

CHAPTER TWELVE

UQUO

A Dolphin dashed towards the bubble, but he was pushed back.

"No good trying fins on it," said Lia. Then she had an idea.

She had kept her lucky feather somewhere. One day, while she had gone for a swim, she found a feather from a Silk, the rarest and most powerful bird in the galaxy!

She had kept it in her drawer back at the shore. She swam up to the shore, crept into her room, grabbed the feather, and ran straight out.

Once again, she jumped headfirst into the water.

The feather was known to have a special ability to empower its user with sharp energy. A matter of seconds later, she emerged from the murky depths, feather in hand.

The crowd of Mertopians stared in awe at the sea serpent behind the girl.

"Pack your bags, people," said the girl. "We're going back to Mermopia!"

The crowd cheered.

PART FIVE

WIND

CHAPTER THIRTEEN

THE PACK

Zac groaned and looked up at the dark sky. He could hear growling in the distance, and as he looked around, he realized that he was surrounded by a pack of storm wolves.

One of the wolves lay on the ground with its red blood oozing out into the moonlight, while a man lay motionless next to it.

Zac realised that he was trapped, and it was all his fault. He had been playing in the wrong area once again—the forbidden forest—and his smell had awakened the sleeping pack.

"Dad, help!" He had cried out, but no one came.

The wolves were about to devour him when he suddenly heard his father's familiar battle cry.

His father had managed to shoot an arrow at one of the wolves and was aiming for the next one when, to Zac's despair, a lone wolf leapt into the air and took a deep bite out of his father's arm.

CHAPTER FOURTEEN

ALL THE BEASTS

Suddenly, the wolves turned around, and Zac did the same. Standing there were four kids around his age. Behind them were four peculiar creatures, all different in color and shape.

Julius, the ice giant,

Zeta, the fire horse,

Mica, the giant mammoth king,

and Uquo, the water serpent.

The pack turned their full attention to the children and attacked.

Julius, Zeta, Mica, and Uquo fought off the wolves like it was just one.

"Who are you?" enquired Zac.

"We were sent here," all four simultaneously said, "to give you this," said Pyro.

Lia handed Zac a sword. There was a thump. Inferno, the wolf king, stood there on two feet, his blood-red eyes gleaming in the dark.

"Engard!" shouted Arnit. Mika obeyed her very command.

He immediately ran towards the wolf. The others joined in too.

They were no match for the king even together. One by one, he tossed them aside.

Zac looked at his sword. On it were the engraved words, "Vortex".

"Vortex!" he screamed. The eye-piercing dragon descended to the ground.

He roared a ferocious roar. A blast of wind knocked the wolf king over. "Engard!" repeated Arnit.

The four beasts all produced a rainbow blast of energy. "Arrgh!" yelled the wolf as it was toppled over.

The cowardly creature got up and scrambled into the sunrise, tail between his legs.

The hologram of a man appeared on Pyro's necklace. "Great job," said the hologram. "And great job to you, young Zac."

Zac looked towards his father, but he was nowhere to be seen. "Your father is in a better place now, Zac," said the wizard. Zac gave a gentle nod.

"This is only the first of our adventures," said Kevin, "and whatever obstacle comes our way next, we will be ready."

The hologram vanished. A loud roar rang through the jungle. "Engard!" said Arnit for the hundredth time.

"You have got to stop saying that," said Lia.

THE

END.

FIVE
BEASTS

JOHN OFON

THIS ADVENTURE JUST GOT MORE EXCITING!

As the first part of 5 Beasts comes to an end, our heroes have defeated the wolf pack and been given an enigmatic gift by four strange beings.

But now that Zac's father's absence has been made public, additional concerns have been raised. What difficulties do our heroes face going forward, and what mysteries do they learn? Join us as we continue our exploration of this enchanted world of exploration and adventure in 5 Beasts season two.

FIVE BEASTS

BEASTS

THE TRAP

JOHN OFON

The heroes now know that Zac's dad might be in trouble. And they're determined to help Zac find his dad safely. As they set out for this new adventure, their overconfidence for their first defeat leads them straight into a trap that almost cost Arnit's life. Find out what happened to Arnit and Zac's dad in part 2…

JOHN OFON

WWW.JOHNOFON.CO.UK

Visit John Ofon's website for more information about the author, Free short stories, Games and more!

Children's Books

Printed in Great Britain
by Amazon